ALSO BY TONI MORRISON

FICTION

The Bluest Eye

Sula

Song of Solomon

Tar Baby

Beloved

Jazz

Paradise

Love

A Mercy

Home

God Help the Child

ESSAYS

Playing in the Dark:
Whiteness and the Literary Imagination

The Origin of Others

The Source of Self-Regard:
Selected Essays, Speeches, and Meditations

Recitatif

Recitatif

A STORY

Toni Morrison

With an Introduction by
Zadie Smith

ALFRED A. KNOPF
New York Toronto
2022

THIS IS A BORZOI BOOK
PUBLISHED BY ALFRED A. KNOPF
AND ALFRED A. KNOPF CANADA

www.aaknopf.com www.penguinrandomhouse.ca

Knopf, Borzoi Books, and the colophon are registered trademarks
of Penguin Random House LLC. Knopf Canada and colophon
are trademarks of Penguin Random House Canada Ltd.

Library of Congress Control Number: 2021944118
ISBN 978-0-593-31503-3 (hardcover)
ISBN 978-0-593-31504-0 (ebook)

Back-of-jacket photograph ©1978 Helen Marcus.
Print: National Portrait Gallery, Smithsonian Institution
Jacket design by John Gall

Manufactured in Canada
Published February 1, 2022
Reprinted One Time
Third Printing, March 2022

Somebody in There After All
by Zadie Smith

In 1980 Toni Morrison sat down to write her one and only short story, "Recitatif." The fact that there *is* only one Morrison short story seems of a piece with her oeuvre. There are no dashed-off Morrison pieces, no filler novels, no treading water, no exit off the main road. There are eleven novels and one short story, all of which she wrote with specific aims and intentions. It's hard to overstate how unusual this is. Most writers work, at least partially, in the dark: subconsciously, stumblingly, progressing chaotically, sometimes taking shortcuts, often reaching dead ends. Morrison was never like that. Perhaps the weight of responsibility she felt herself to be under did not allow for it. To read the startlingly detailed auto-critiques of her own novels in that last book, *The Source of Self-Regard,* was to observe a literary lab technician reverse-engineering an experiment. And it is this mixture of poetic form and scientific method in Morrison that is, to my mind, unique. Certainly it makes any exercise in close reading her work intensely rewarding, for you can feel fairly certain—page by page, line by line—that nothing has been left to chance, least of all the originating intention. With "Recitatif" she was explicit. This extraordinary story you hold in your hands was specifically intended as "an experiment in the removal of all racial codes from a narrative about two characters of different races for whom racial identity is crucial." *

THE CHARACTERS IN QUESTION are Twyla and Roberta, two poor girls, eight years old and wards of the state, who spend four months together in St. Bonaventure shelter. The very first thing we learn about them, from Twyla, is this: "My mother danced all night and Roberta's was sick." A little later, that they were placed together, in room 406, "stuck in a strange place with

* Toni Morrison, preface to *Playing in the Dark: Whiteness and the Literary Imagination* (New York: Vintage, 1993), xi.

a girl from a whole other race." What we never learn definitively—no matter how closely we read—is which of these girls is black and which white. We will assume, we can insist, but can't be sure. And this despite the fact that we get to see them grow up, becoming adults who occasionally run into each other. We eavesdrop when they speak, examine their clothes, hear of their husbands, their jobs, their children, their lives . . . The crucial detail is withheld. A puzzle of a story, then—a game. Only, Toni Morrison does not play. When she called "Recitatif" an "experiment" she meant it. The subject of the experiment is the reader.

BUT BEFORE GOING any further into the ingenious design of this philosophical* brain teaser, the title itself is worth a good, long look:

Recitatif, recitative | ˌrɛsɪtəˈtiːv | noun *[mass noun]*

1. Musical declamation of the kind usual in the narrative and dialogue parts of opera and oratorio,

---

* I have no idea if Morrison ever read the philosopher John Rawls, but the overlap between the premise of "Recitatif" and the structure of Rawls's "veil of ignorance" is intriguing.

sung in the rhythm of ordinary speech with many words on the same note: *singing in recitative.*

2. The tone or rhythm peculiar to any language *obs*

The music of Morrison begins in "ordinary speech." Her ear was acute, and rescuing African American speech patterns from the debasements of the American mainstream is a defining feature of her early work. In this story, though, the challenge of capturing "ordinary speech" has been deliberately complicated. For many words are here to be "sung on the same note." That is, we will hear the words of Twyla and the words of Roberta, and although they are perfectly differentiated the one from the other, we will not be able to differentiate them in the *one way we really want to*. An experiment easy to imagine but difficult to execute. In order to make it work, you'd need to write in such a way that every phrase precisely straddled the line between characteristically "black" and "white" American speech, and that's a high-wire act in an eagle-eyed country, ever alert to racial codes, adept at categorization, in which most people feel they can spot a black or white speaker with their eyes closed, precisely because of the tone and rhythm "peculiar to" their language . . .

And beyond language, in a racialized system, all manner of things will read as "peculiar to" one kind of person or another. The food a character eats, the music they like, where they live, how they work. Black things, white things. Things that are peculiar to our people and peculiar to theirs. But one of the questions of "Recitatif" is precisely what that phrase "peculiar to" really signifies. For we tend to use it variously, not realizing that we do. It can mean:

That which *characterizes*
That which *belongs exclusively to*
That which *is an essential quality of*

These three are not the same. The first suggests a tendency; the second implies some form of ownership; the third speaks of essences and therefore of immutable natural laws. In "Recitatif" these differences prove crucial, as we will see.

MUCH OF THE MESMERIZING POWER of "Recitatif" lies in that first definition of "peculiar to": *that which characterizes*. As readers we urgently want to characterize the various characteristics on display. But how? *My mother danced all night and Roberta's was sick.* Well, now, what kind of mother tends to dance all night? A black one or a white one? And whose mother is more likely to be sick? Is Roberta a blacker name than Twyla? Or vice versa? And what about voice? Twyla narrates it in the first person, and so we may have the commonsense feeling that *she* must be the black girl, for her author is black. But it doesn't take much interrogating of this "must" to realize it rests on rather shallow, autobiographical ideas of authorship that would seem wholly unworthy of the complex experiment that has been set before us. Besides, Morrison was never a poor child in a state institution—she grew up solidly working-class in integrated Lorain, Ohio—and autobiography was never a very strong element of her work. Her imagination was capacious. No, autobiography will not get us very far here. So, we listen a little more closely to Twyla:

> And Mary, that's my mother, she was right. Every now and then she would stop dancing long enough to tell me something important and one of the things she said was that they never washed their hair and they smelled funny. Roberta sure did. Smell funny, I mean. So when the Big Bozo (nobody ever called her Mrs. Itkin, just like nobody ever said St. Bonaventure)—when she said, "Twyla, this is Roberta. Roberta, this is Twyla. Make each other

welcome," I said, "My mother won't like you putting me in here."

The game is afoot. Morrison bypasses any detail that might imply an *essential quality of*, slyly evades whatever would *belong exclusively to* one girl or the other, and makes us sit instead in this uncomfortable, double-dealing world of *that which characterizes,* in which Twyla seems to move in a moment from black to white to black again, depending on the nature of your perception. Like that dress on the Internet no one could ever agree on the color of . . .

WHEN READING "Recitatif" with students, there is a moment where the class grows uncomfortable at their own eagerness to settle the question, maybe because most attempts to answer it tend to reveal more about the reader than the character.* For example: Twyla loves the food at St. Bonaventure and Roberta hates it. (The food is Spam, Salisbury steak, Jell-O with fruit cocktail in it.) Is Twyla black? Twyla's mother's idea

---

* In "Black Writing, White Reading: Race and the Politics of Feminist Interpretation," the literary critic Elizabeth Abel claims that most white readers read Twyla as white, while most black readers will see Twyla as black.

of supper is "popcorn and a can of Yoo-hoo." Is Twyla white?

Twyla's mother looks like this:

> She had on those green slacks I hated. . . . And that fur jacket with the pocket linings so ripped she had to pull to get her hands out of them. . . . [But] she looked so beautiful even in those ugly green slacks that made her behind stick out.

Roberta's mother looks like this:

> She was big. Bigger than any man and on her chest was the biggest cross I'd ever seen. I swear it was six inches long each way. And in the crook of her arm was the biggest Bible ever made.

Does that help? We might think the puzzle is solved when both mothers come to visit their daughters one Sunday and Roberta's mother refuses to shake Twyla's mother's hand. But a moment later, upon reflection, it will strike us that a pious, upstanding, sickly black mother might be just as unlikely to shake the hand of an immoral, fast-living, trashy, dancing white mother as vice versa . . . Complicating matters further, Twyla and Roberta—despite their crucial differences—seem to share the same low status within the confines of St. Bonaventure. Or at least, that's how Twyla sees it:

> We didn't like each other all that much at first, but nobody else wanted to play with us because we weren't real orphans with beautiful dead parents in the sky. We were dumped. Even the New York City Puerto Ricans and the upstate Indians ignored us.

At this point, many readers will start getting a little desperate to put back in precisely what Morrison has deliberately removed. You start combing the fine print:

> We were eight years old and got F's all the time. Me because I couldn't remember what I read or what the teacher said. And Roberta because she couldn't read at all and didn't even listen to the teacher.

Which version of educational failure is more black? Which kind of poor people eat so poorly—or are so grateful to eat bad food? Poor black folk or poor white folk? Both?

As a reader you know there's something unseemly in these kinds of inquiries but old habits die hard. You *need* to know. So you try another angle. You get granular.

a. Twyla's mother brings no food for her daughter on that Sunday outing
b. Cries out "Twyla, baby!" when she spots her in the chapel
c. Is pretty
d. Smells of Lady Esther dusting powder
e. Doesn't wear a hat in a house of God
f. Calls Roberta's mum "that bitch!" and "twitched and crossed and uncrossed her legs all through service."

Meanwhile, Roberta's mother brings plenty of food—which Roberta refuses—but says not a word to anyone, although she does read aloud to Roberta from the Bible. There's a lot of readable difference there, and Twyla certainly notices it all:

Things are not right. The wrong food is always with the wrong people. Maybe that's why I got into waitress work later—to match up the right people with the right food.

She seems jealous. But can vectors of longing, resentment or desire tell us who's who? Is Twyla a black girl jealous of a white mother who brought more food? Or a white girl resentful of a black mother who thinks she's too godly to shake hands?

CHILDREN ARE CURIOUS about justice. Sometimes they are shocked by their encounters with its opposite. They say to themselves: *Things are not right.* But children also experiment with injustice, with cruelty. To stress-test the structure of the adult world. To find out exactly what its rules are. (The fact that questions of justice seem an inconvenient speculation for so many adults cannot go unnoticed by children.) And it is when reflecting upon a moment of childish cruelty that Twyla begins to describe a different binary altogether. Not the familiar one that divides black and white, but the one between those who live within the system—whatever their position may be within it—and those who are cast far outside of it. The unspeakable. The outcast. The forgotten. The nobody. Because there *is* a person in St. Bonaventure whose position is lower than either Twyla's or Roberta's—far lower. Her name is Maggie:

> The kitchen woman with legs like parentheses. . . .
> Maggie couldn't talk. The kids said she had her
> tongue cut out, but I think she was just born that
> way: mute. She was old and sandy colored and she

worked in the kitchen. I don't know if she was nice or not. I just remember her legs like parentheses and how she rocked when she walked.

Maggie has no characteristic language. She has no language at all. Once she fell over in the school orchard and the older girls laughed and Twyla and Roberta did nothing. She is not a person you can do things for: she is only an object of ridicule. "She wore this really stupid little hat—a kid's hat with earflaps—and she wasn't much taller than we were." In the social system of St. Bonaventure, Maggie stands outside all hierarchies. She's one to whom anything can be said. One to whom anything might be done. Like a slave. Which is what it means to be nobody. Twyla and Roberta, noticing this, take a childish interest in what it means to be nobody:

"But what about if somebody tries to kill her?" I used to wonder about that. "Or what if she wants to cry. Can she cry?"

"Sure," Roberta said. "But just tears. No sounds come out."

"She can't scream?"

"Nope. Nothing."

"Can she hear?"

"I guess."

"Let's call her," I said. And we did.

"Dummy! Dummy!" She never turned her head.

"Bow legs! Bow legs!" Nothing. She just rocked on, the chin straps of her baby-boy hat swaying from side to side. I think we were wrong. I think she could hear and didn't let on. And it shames me even now to think there was somebody in there after all who heard us call her those names and couldn't tell on us.

TIME LEAPS FORWARD. Roberta leaves St. Bonny's first, and a few months after so does Twyla. The girls grow into women. Years later, Twyla is waitressing at an upstate Howard Johnson's, when who should walk in but Roberta, just in time to give us some more racial cues to debate.* These days Roberta's hair is "so big and wild" Twyla can barely see her face. She's wearing a halter and hot pants and sitting between two hirsute guys with big hair and beards. She seems to be on

---

* Although some writerly types might here want to take a break from the exhausting business of racial profiling to admire the elegance and economy with which Morrison sets scenes and moods, in this case, the feeling of working the early shift at a roadside restaurant: *Very light until a Greyhound checked in for breakfast around six-thirty. At that hour the sun was all the way clear of the hills behind the restaurant. The place looked better at night—more like shelter—but I loved it when the sun broke in, even if it did show all the cracks in the vinyl.*

drugs. Now, Roberta and friends are going to see Hendrix, and would any other artist have worked quite so well for Morrison's purpose? Hendrix's hair is big and wild. Is his music black or white? Your call. Either way, Twyla—her own hair "shapeless in a net"—has never heard of him, and when she says she lives in Newburgh, Roberta laughs.

GEOGRAPHY, IN AMERICA, is fundamental to racial codes, and Newburgh—sixty miles north of Manhattan—is an archetypal racialized American city. Founded in 1709, it is where Washington announced the cessation of hostilities with Britain and therefore the beginning of America as a nation, and in the nineteenth century was a grand and booming town, with a growing black middle class. The Second World War manufacturing boom brought waves of African American migrants into Newburgh, eager to escape the racial terrorism of the South, looking for low-wage work, but with the end of the war the work dried up; factory jobs were relocated south or abroad, and by the time Morrison wrote "Recitatif," Newburgh was a depressed town, hit by "white flight," riven with poverty and the violence that attends poverty, and with large sections of its once beautiful waterfront bulldozed in the name of "urban renewal." Twyla is married to a Newburgh man from an old Newburgh family, whose race the reader is invited to decipher ("James and his father talk about fishing and baseball and I can see them all together on the Hudson in a raggedy skiff") but who is certainly one of the millions of twentieth-century Americans who watched once thriving towns mismanaged and abandoned by the federal government: "Half the population of Newburgh is on welfare now, but to my husband's family it was still some upstate paradise of a time long past." And then, when the town is on its knees, and the great houses empty and abandoned, and downtown a wasteland of empty shopfronts and aimless kids on the corner—the new money moves in. The old houses get done up. A Food Emporium opens. And it's in this Emporium—twelve years after their last run-in—that the women meet again, but this time all is transformation. Roberta's cleaned up her act and married a rich man:

> Shoes, dress, everything lovely and summery and rich. I was dying to know what happened to her, how she got from Jimi Hendrix to Annandale, a neighborhood full of doctors and IBM executives.

Easy, I thought. Everything is so easy for them. They think they own the world.

For the reader determined to solve the puzzle—the reader who believes the puzzle can be solved, or must be solved—this is surely exhibit number one. Everything hangs on that word "they." To whom is it pointing? Uppity black people? Entitled white people? Rich people, whatever their color? Gentrifiers? You choose.

NOT TOO LONG AGO, I happened to be in Annandale myself, standing in the post office line, staring absently at the list of national holidays fixed to the wall, and reflecting that the only uncontested date in the American calendar is New Year's Day. With Twyla and Roberta, it's the same—every element of their shared past is contested:

> "Oh, Twyla, you know how it was in those days: black-white. You know how everything was."
> But I didn't know. I thought it was just the opposite. . . . You got to see everything at Howard Johnson's and blacks were very friendly with whites in those days.

Their most contested site is Maggie. Maggie is their Columbus Day, their Thanksgiving. What the hell happened to Maggie? At the beginning of "Recitatif," we are informed that sandy-colored Maggie "fell" down. Later, Roberta insists she was knocked down, by the older girls—an event Twyla does not remember. Later still, Roberta claims Maggie was black and that Twyla pushed her down, which sparks an epistemological crisis in Twyla, who does not remember Maggie being black, never mind pushing her. ("I wouldn't forget a thing like that. Would I?") Then Roberta claims they *both* pushed and kicked "a black lady who couldn't even scream." It's interesting to note that this escalation of claims happens at a moment of national "racial strife," in the form of school bussing. Both Roberta's and Twyla's children are being sent far across town. And as black—or white—mothers, the two find themselves in rigid positions, on either side of a literal boundary: a protest line. Their shared past starts to fray and then morph under the weight of a mutual anger; even the tiniest things are reinterpreted. They used to like doing each other's hair, as kids. Now Twyla rejects this commonality (*I hated your hands in my hair*) and Roberta rejects any possibility of alliance with Twyla, in favor of the group identity of the other mothers who feel about bussing as she does.*

The personal connection they once made can hardly be expected to withstand a situation in which once again race proves socially determinant, and in one of the most vulnerable sites any of us have: the education of our children. Mutual suspicion blooms. Why should I trust this person? What are they trying to take from me? My culture? My community? My schools? My neighborhood? My life? Positions get entrenched. Nothing can be shared. Twyla and Roberta start carrying increasingly extreme signs at competing protests. (Twyla: "My signs got crazier each day.") A hundred and forty characters or less: that's about as much as you can fit on a homemade sign. Both women find ad hominem attacks work best. You could say they are never as far apart as at this moment of "racial strife." You could also say they are in lockstep, for without the self-definition offered by the binary they appear meaningless, even to them-

---

* At this point—true to type!—I was pretty certain Twyla was black. I could hear potential class solidarity in these lines: "I thought it was a good thing until I heard it was a bad thing. I mean I didn't know. All the schools seemed dumps to me." And this, I thought, is precisely what Roberta rejects, in favor of retaining the high position in the social hierarchy that both her race and now her money provide. But if Twyla's black, could she possibly forget that Maggie was, too? Back to square one. Or back to square one AND square zero, that paradoxical, shimmering field beyond the binary. Can we imagine any of our struggles for justice being made from this place?

selves. ("Actually my sign didn't make sense without Roberta's.")

AS TWYLA AND ROBERTA DISCOVER, it's hard to admit a shared humanity with your neighbor if they will not come with you to reexamine a shared history. Such reexaminations I sometimes hear described as "resentment politics," as if telling a history in full could *only be* the product of a personal resentment, rather than a necessary act performed in the service of curiosity, interest, understanding (of both self and community), and justice itself. But some people sure do take it personal. I couldn't help but smile to read of an ex–newspaper editor from my country, who, when speaking of his discomfort at recent efforts to reveal the slave history behind many of our great country houses, complained, "I think comfort does matter. I know people say, 'Oh, we must be uncomfortable.' . . . Why should I pay a hundred quid a year, or whatever, to be told what a shit I am?" Imagine thinking of history this way! As a thing *personally directed at you.* As a series of events structured to make you *feel* one way or another, rather than the precondition of all our lives?

The long, bloody, tangled encounter between the European peoples and the African continent *is* our history. Our shared history. It's what happened. It's not the moral equivalent of a football game where your "side" wins or loses. To give an account of an old English country house that includes not only the provenance of the beautiful paintings but also the provenance of the money that bought them—who suffered and died making that money, how, and why—is history told in full and should surely be of interest to everybody, black or white or neither. And I admit I *do* begin to feel resentment—actually, something closer to fury—when I realize that merely speaking such facts aloud is so discomfiting to some that they'd rather deny the facts themselves. For the sake of peaceful relations. To better forget about it. To better move on. Many people have this instinct. Twyla and Roberta also want to forget and move on. They want to blame it on the "gar girls," or on each other, or on faulty memory itself. *Maggie was black. Maggie was white. They hurt Maggie. You did.* But by the end of "Recitatif," they are both ready to at least try and discuss "what the hell happened to Maggie." Not for the shallow motive of transhistorical blame, much less to induce personal comfort or discomfort, but rather in the service of truth. We know their exploration of the question will be painful, messy, and very likely never perfectly settled. But we also know that a good-faith attempt is better than its opposite. Which would be to go on pretending, as Twyla puts it, that "everything was hunky-dory."

DIFFICULT TO "MOVE ON" from any site of suffering if that suffering goes unacknowledged and undescribed. Citizens from Belfast and Belgrade know this, in Berlin and Banjul. (And that's just the B's.) In the privacy of our domestic arguments we know this. We *must* be heard. It's human to want to be heard. We are nobody if not heard. *I suffered. They suffered. My people suffered! My people continue to suffer!* Some take the narrowest possible view of this category of "my people": they mean only their immediate family. For others, the cry widens out to encompass a city, a nation, a faith group, a perceived racial category, a diaspora. But whatever your personal allegiances, when you deliberately turn from any human suffering you make what should be a porous border between "your people" and the rest of humanity into something rigid and deadly. You ask not to be bothered by the history of nobodies, the suffering of nobodies. (Or the suffering of somebodies, if hierarchical reversal is your jam.) But surely the very least we can do is listen to what was done to a person—or is still being done. It is the very least we owe the dead, and the suffering. People suffered to build this house, to found that bank, or your country. Maggie suffered at St. Bonaventure. And all we have to do is *hear* about that? How *can* we resent it?*

It takes Twyla some time to see past her resentment at being offered a new version of a past she thought she knew. ("Roberta had messed up my past somehow with that business about Maggie. I wouldn't forget a thing like that. Would I?") But in her forced reconsideration of a shared history, she comes to a deeper realization about her own motives:

> I didn't kick her; I didn't join in with the gar girls and kick that lady, but I sure did want to. We watched and never tried to help her and never called for help. Maggie was my dancing mother. Deaf, I thought, and dumb. Nobody inside. Nobody who would hear you if you cried in the night. . . . And when the gar

---

* The fear is that hearing about it will inevitably lead to doing something about it, and panics about restitution and reparations are usually couched in the terms of "revenge." Rarely do we think of restitution not as a *taking from* but as an *adding to*, as a potential enrichment for everybody. Yet, in other contexts, we do seem capable of such a thought. The postwar GI Bill, for example—which was a form of reparation for a particular group of people, and succeeded in educating thousands of working-class Americans—became a great wealth, both cultural and economic, not just for individuals but, over the longer term, for America itself.

girls pushed her down, and started roughhousing, I knew she wouldn't scream, couldn't—just like me and I was glad about that.

A few pages later, Roberta spontaneously comes to a similar conclusion (although she is now unsure as to whether or not Maggie was, indeed, black). I find the above one of the most stunning paragraphs in all of Morrison's work. The psychological subtlety of it. The mix of projection, vicarious action, self-justification, sadistic pleasure, and personal trauma that she identifies as a motivating force within Twyla, and that, by extrapolation, she prompts us to recognize in ourselves.

LIKE TWYLA, Morrison wants us ashamed of how we treat the powerless, even if we, too, feel powerless. And one of the ethical complexities of "Recitatif" is the uncomfortable fact that even as Twyla and Roberta fight to assert their own identities—the fact they are both "somebody"—they simultaneously cast others into the role of nobodies. The "fags who wanted company" in the chapel are nobodies to them, and they are so repelled by and fixated upon Maggie's disability they see nothing else about her. But there is somebody in all these people, after all. There is somebody in all of us.

This fact is our shared experience, our shared category: the human. Which acknowledgment is often misused or only half used, employed as a form of sentimental or aesthetic contemplation, i.e., *Oh, though we seem so unalike, how alike we all are under our skins . . .* But, historically, this acknowledgment of the human—our inescapable shared category—has also played a role in the work of freedom riders, abolitionists, anticolonialists, trade unionists, queer activists, suffragettes, and in the thoughts of the likes of Frantz Fanon, Malcolm X, Stuart Hall, Paul Gilroy, Morrison herself. If it is a humanism, it is a radical one, which struggles toward solidarity in alterity, the possibility and promise of unity across difference. When applied to racial matters, it recognizes that although the category of race is both experientially and structurally "real," it yet has no ultimate or essential reality in and of itself.[*]

BUT, OF COURSE, ultimate reality is not where any of us live. For hundreds of years, we have lived in

---

[*] As Siddhartha Mukherjee points out in his book *The Gene: An Intimate History,* the overwhelming proportion of genetic diversity (85 to 90 percent) occurs within so-called races (i.e., within Asians or Africans) rather than between them. Which means there's more "racial" difference between a man from Nigeria and a man from Namibia than between a "white" man and a "black" one.

deliberately racialized human structures—that is to say, socially pervasive and sometimes legally binding fictions—that prove incapable of stating difference and equality simultaneously. And it is extremely galling to hear you have suffered for a fiction, or indeed profited from one. It has been fascinating to watch the recent panicked response to the interrogation of whiteness, the terror at the dismantling of a false racial category that for centuries united the rich man born and raised in Belarus, say, with the poor woman born and raised in Wales, under the shared banner of racial superiority. But panic is not entirely absent on the other side of the binary. If race is a construct, what will happen to blackness? Can the categories of black music and black literature survive? What would the phrase "black joy" signify? How can we throw out this dirty bathwater of racism when for centuries we have pressed the baby of race so close to our hearts, and made—even accounting for all the horror—so many beautiful things with it?

TONI MORRISON LOVED the culture and community of the African diaspora in America, even—especially—those elements that were forged as response and defense against the dehumanizing violence of slavery, the political humiliations of Reconstruction, the brutal segregation and state terrorism of Jim Crow, and the many civil rights successes and neoliberal disappointments that have followed. Out of this history she made a literature, a shelf of books that—for as long as they are read—will serve to remind America that its story about itself was always partial and self-deceiving. And here, for many people, we reach an impasse: a dead end. If race is a construct, whither blackness? If whiteness is an illusion, on what else can a poor man without prospects pride himself? I think a lot of people's brains actually break at this point. But Morrison had a bigger brain. She could parse the difference between the deadness of a determining category and the richness of a lived experience. And there are some clues in this story, I think. Some hints at alternative ways of conceptualizing difference without either erasing or codifying it. Surprising civic values, fresh philosophical principles. Not only categorization and visibility but also privacy and kindness:

> Now we were behaving like sisters separated for much too long. Those four short months were nothing in time. Maybe it was the thing itself. Just being there, together. Two little girls who knew what nobody else in the world knew—how not to ask questions. How to believe what had to be believed.

There was politeness in that reluctance and generosity as well. Is your mother sick too? No, she dances all night. Oh—and an understanding nod.

That people live and die within a specific history—within deeply embedded cultural, racial, and class codes—is a reality that cannot be denied, and often a beautiful one. It's what creates difference. But there are ways to deal with that difference that are expansive and comprehending, rather than narrow and diagnostic. Instead of only ticking boxes on doctors' forms—pathologizing difference—we might also take a compassionate and discreet interest in it. We don't always have to judge difference or categorize it or criminalize it. We don't have to take it personally. We can also just let it be. Or we can, like Morrison, be profoundly interested in it:

> The struggle was for writing that was indisputably black. I don't yet know quite what that is, but neither that nor the attempts to disqualify an effort to find out keeps me from trying to pursue it.
>
> My choices of language (speakerly, aural, colloquial), my reliance for full comprehension on codes embedded in black culture, my effort to effect immediate co-conspiracy and intimacy (without any

distancing, explanatory fabric), as well as my attempt to shape a silence while breaking it are attempts to transfigure the complexity and wealth of Black American culture into a language worthy of the culture.*

Visibility and privacy, communication and silence, intimacy and encounter are all expressed here. The reader who sees only their own exclusion in this paragraph may need to mentally perform, in their own minds, the experiment "Recitatif" performs in fiction: *the removal of all racial codes from a narrative about two characters of different races for whom racial identity is crucial.* To perform this experiment in a literary space, I will choose, for my other character, another Nobel Prize winner, Seamus Heaney. I am looking at his poems. I am looking in. To fully comprehend Heaney's oeuvre, I would have to be wholly embedded in the codes of Northern Irish culture; I am not. No more than I am wholly embedded in the African American culture out of which and toward which Morrison writes. I am not a perfect co-conspirator of either writer. I had to google to find out what "Lady Esther dusting powder" is in "Recitatif," and when Heaney mentions hoard-

* Toni Morrison, foreword to *The Bluest Eye* (New York: Vintage Books), xii–xiii.

ing "fresh berries in the byre," no image comes to my mind.* As a reader of these two embedded writers, both profoundly interested in their own communities, I can only be a thrilled observer, always partially included—by that great shared category, the human—but also simultaneously on the outside looking in, enriched by that which is new or alien to me, especially when it has not been diluted or falsely presented to flatter my ignorance—that dreaded "explanatory fabric." Instead, they both keep me rigorous company on the page, not begging for my comprehension but always open to the possibility of it, for no writer would break a silence if they did not want someone—some always unknowable someone—to overhear. I am describing a model reader-writer relationship. But as "Recitatif" suggests, the same values expressed here might also prove useful to us in our roles as citizens, allies, friends.

RACE, FOR MANY, is a determining brand, simply one side of a rigid binary. Blackness, as Morrison conceived

---

* And then there are those times when writers on opposite sides of the binary seem, as in a recitatif, to be momentarily singing different words on the same note. As here, in "Clearances," where Heaney describes code-switching so he can speak to his own mother:

> I'd *naw* and *aye*
> And decently relapse into the wrong
> Grammar which kept us allied and at bay.

of it, was a shared history, an experience, a culture, a language. A complexity, a wealth. To believe in black-ness solely as a negative binary in a prejudicial racial-ized structure, and to further believe that this binary is and will forever be the essential, eternal, and *primary* organizing category of human life, is a pessimist's right but an activist's indulgence. Meanwhile, there is work to be done. And what is the purpose of all this work if our positions within prejudicial, racialized structures are permanent, essential, unchangeable—as rigid as the rules of gravity?

The forces of capital, meanwhile, are pragmatic: capital does not bother itself with essentialisms. It trans-forms nobodies into somebodies—and vice versa—depending on where the labor is needed and the profit can be made. The Irish became somebodies when in-dentured labor had to be formally differentiated from slavery, to justify the latter category. In Britain, we only decided that there was something inside women—or enough of a something to be able to vote with—in the early twentieth century. British women went from being essentially angels of the house—whose essential nature was considered to be domestic—to nodes in a system whose essential nature was to work, just like men, although we were welcome to pump milk in the office basement if we really had to ... Yes, capital is adaptive, pragmatic. It is always looking for new markets, new sites of economic vulnerability, of potential exploitation—new Maggies. New human beings whose essential nature is to be nobody. We claim to know this even as we simultaneously misremember or elide the many Maggies in our own lives. These days Roberta—or Twyla—might march for women's rights, all the while wearing a four-dollar T-shirt, product of the enforced labor of Uyghur women on the other side of the world. Twyla—or Roberta—could go door to door, registering voters, while sporting long nails freshly painted by a trafficked young girl. Roberta—or Twyla—may practice "self-care" by going to the hairdresser to get extensions shorn from another, poorer woman's head. Far beneath the "black-white" racial strife of America, there persists a global underclass of Maggies, unseen and unconsidered within the parochial American conversation, the wretched of the earth . . .

OUR RACIAL CODES ARE "peculiar to" us, but what do we really mean by that? In "Recitatif," that which would *characterize* Twyla and Roberta as black or white is the consequence of history, of shared experience, and what shared histories inevitably produce: culture, community, identity. What belongs *exclusively* to them is their subjective experience of these same categories in which they have lived. Some of these experiences will have been nourishing, joyful, and beautiful; many others prejudicial, exploitative, and punitive. No one can take a person's subjective experiences from them. No one should try. Whether Twyla or Roberta is the somebody who has lived within the category of "white" we cannot be sure, but Morrison constructs the story in such a way that we are forced to admit the fact that other categories, aside from the racial, also produce shared experiences. Categories like being poor, being female, like being at the mercy of the state or the police, like living in a certain zip code, having children, hating your mother, wanting the best for your family. We are like and not like a lot of people a lot of the time. White may be the most powerful category in the racial hierarchy, but if you're an eight-year-old girl in a state institution with a delinquent mother and no money, it sure doesn't feel that way. Black may be the lower caste, but if you marry an IBM guy and have two servants and a driver, you are—at the very least—in a new position in relation to the least powerful people in your society. And vice versa. Life is complex, conceptually dominated by binaries but never wholly contained by them. Morrison is the great master of American complexity, and "Recitatif," in my view, sits alongside "Bartleby, the Scrivener" and "The Lottery" as a perfect—and perfectly American—tale, one every American child should read.

Finally, what is *essentially* black or white about Twyla and Roberta I believe we bring to "Recitatif" ourselves, within a system of signs over which too many humans have collectively labored for hundreds of years now. It began in the racialized system of capitalism we call slavery; it was preserved in law long after slavery ended, and continues to assert itself, to sometimes lethal effect, in social, economic, educational, and judicial systems all over the world. But as a category the fact remains that it has no objective reality: it is not, like gravity, a principle of the earth. By removing it from the story, Morrison reveals both the speciousness of "black-white" as our primary human categorization and its dehumanizing effect on human life. But she also lovingly demonstrates how much meaning we were able to find—and continue to find—in our beloved categories. The peculiar way our people make this or that dish, the peculiar music we play at a cookout or a funeral, the peculiar way we use nouns or adjectives, the peculiar way we walk or dance or paint or write— these things are dear to us. Especially if denigrated by others, we will tend to hold them close. We feel they define us. And this form of self-regard, for Morrison, was the road back to the human—the insistence that you are somebody although the structures you have lived within have categorized you as "nobody." The direct descendant of slaves, Morrison writes in a way that recognizes first—and primarily—the somebody within black people, the black human having been, historically, the ultimate example of the dehumanized subject: the one literally transformed, by capital, from subject to object. But in this lifelong project, as the critic Jesse McCarthy has pointed out, we are invited to see a foundation for all social justice movements: "The battle over the meaning of black humanity has always been central to both [Toni Morrison's] fiction and essays—and not just for the sake of black people but to further what we hope all of humanity can become." * We hope all of humanity will reject the project of dehumanization. We hope for a literature—and a society!—that recognizes the somebody in everybody. This despite the fact that in America's zero-sum game of racialized capitalism, this form of humanism has been abandoned as an apolitical quantity, toothless, an inanity to repeat,

* Jesse McCarthy, "The Origin of Others," in *Who Will Pay Reparations on My Soul?* (New York: Liveright, 2021), 30.

perhaps, on *Sesame Street* ("Everybody's somebody!") but considered too naïve and insufficient a basis for radical change.[*]

I HAVE WRITTEN a lot in this essay about prejudicial structures. But I've spoken vaguely of them, metaphorically, as a lot of people do these days. In an address to Howard University in 1995, Morrison got specific. She broke it down, in her scientific way. It is a very useful summary, to be cut out and kept for future reference, for if we hope to dismantle oppressive structures it will surely help to examine how they are built:

> Let us be reminded that before there is a final solution, there must be a first solution, a second one, even a third. The move toward a final solution is not

[*] A persuasive counterargument to the radical humanist case is the idea that power itself is sadistic: it doesn't want to hurt "nobodies." It *wants* to torture somebody. To the sadist, there's no satisfaction in whipping a man if you don't know that he's a human being, just like you, and capable of suffering, just like you. And reading of plantation overseers, gulag chiefs, and Nazi guards, what student of history can doubt the existence of precisely this form of psychotic sadism? But the question remains: How common is it? What surely *is* common, in the general population, is complicity, silence, prejudice, and the desire not to be made uncomfortable by the sufferings of others. The most common contemporaneous response to the horrors of the plantation, gulag, or concentration camp was indifference.

a jump. It takes one step, then another, then another. Something, perhaps, like this:

1. Construct an internal enemy, as both focus and diversion.

2. Isolate and demonize that enemy by unleashing and protecting the utterance of overt and coded name-calling and verbal abuse. Employ ad hominem attacks as legitimate charges against that enemy.

3. Enlist and create sources and distributors of information who are willing to reinforce the demonizing process because it is profitable, because it grants power, and because it works.

4. Palisade all art forms; monitor, discredit, or expel those that challenge or destabilize processes of demonization and deification.

5. Subvert and malign all representatives of and sympathizers with this constructed enemy.

6. Solicit, from among the enemy, collaborators who agree with and can sanitize the dispossession process.

7. Pathologize the enemy in scholarly and popular mediums; recycle, for example, scientific racism and the myths of racial superiority in order to naturalize the pathology.

8. Criminalize the enemy. Then prepare, bud-

get for, and rationalize the building of holding arenas for the enemy—especially its males and absolutely its children.

9. Reward mindlessness and apathy with monumentalized entertainments and with little pleasures, tiny seductions: a few minutes on television, a few lines in the press, a little pseudo-success, the illusion of power and influence; a little fun, a little style, a little consequence.

10. Maintain, at all costs, silence.*

Elements of this fascist playbook can be seen in the European encounter with Africa, between the West and the East, between the rich and the poor, between the Germans and the Jews, the Hutus and the Tutsis, the British and the Irish, the Serbs and the Croats. It is one of our continual human possibilities. Racism is a kind of fascism, perhaps the most pernicious and long-lasting. But it is still a man-made structure. The capacity for fascisms of one kind or another is something else we all share—you might call it our most depressing collective identity. (And if we are currently engaged in trying to effect change, it could be worthwhile—as an act of ethical spring-cleaning—

* Toni Morrison, "Racism and Fascism," in *The Source of Self-Regard* (New York: Vintage Books, 2020), 14–15.

checking through Toni's list and ensuring we are not employing any of the playbook of fascism in our own work.) Fascism labors to create the category of the "nobody," the scapegoat, the sufferer. Morrison repudiated that category as it has applied to black people over centuries, and in doing so strengthened the category of the "somebody" for all of us, whether black or white or neither. Othering whoever has othered us, in reverse, is no liberation—as cathartic as it may feel.* Liberation is liberation: the recognition of somebody in everybody.†

---

* Hierarchical reversals do not seem to have interested Morrison very much. Here she is with a surprising take on the term "feminist" in a 1998 *Salon* interview:

> "I would never write any 'ist.' I don't write 'ist' novels. . . . I can't take positions that are closed. Everything I've ever done, in the writing world, has been to expand articulation, rather than to close it, to open doors, sometimes, not even closing the book—leaving the endings open for reinterpretation, revisitation, a little ambiguity. I detest and loathe [those categories]. I think it's off-putting to some readers, who may feel that I'm involved in writing some kind of feminist tract. I don't subscribe to patriarchy, and I don't think it should be substituted with matriarchy. I think it's a question of equitable access, and opening doors to all sorts of things."

† In a 1998 introductory essay to a new edition of *The Bluest Eye,* Morrison makes this point when she explains why she resisted "othering" the characters who have othered Pecola Breedlove: "Singular as Pecola's life was, I believed some aspects of her woundability were lodged in all young girls. In exploring the social and domestic aggression that could cause a child to literally fall apart, I mounted a series of rejections, some routine, some exceptional, some monstrous, all the while trying hard *to avoid complicity in the demonization process Pecola was subjected to. That is, I did not want to dehumanize the characters who trashed Pecola and contributed to her collapse.*" (My italics.)

. . .

STILL, LIKE MOST READERS of "Recitatif," I found it impossible not to hunger to know who the other was, Twyla or Roberta. Oh, I urgently wanted to have it straightened out. Wanted to sympathize warmly in one sure place, turn cold in the other. To feel for the somebody and dismiss the nobody. But this is precisely what Morrison *deliberately and methodically will not allow me to do.* It's worth asking ourselves why. "Recitatif" reminds me that it is not essentially black or white to be poor, oppressed, lesser than, exploited, ignored. The answer to "What the hell happened to Maggie?" is not written in the stars, or in the blood, or in the genes, or forever predetermined by history. Whatever was done to Maggie was done by people. People like Twyla and Roberta. People like you and me.

.

Recitatif

M Y MOTHER DANCED all night and Roberta's was sick. That's why we were taken to St. Bonny's. People want to put their arms around you when you tell them you were in a shelter, but it really wasn't bad. No big long room with one hundred beds like Bellevue. There were four to a room, and when Roberta and me came, there was a shortage of state kids, so we were the only ones assigned to 406 and could go from bed to bed if we wanted to. And we wanted to, too. We changed beds every night and for the whole four months we were there we never picked one out as our own permanent bed.

It didn't start out that way. The minute I walked

in and the Big Bozo introduced us, I got sick to my stomach. It was one thing to be taken out of your own bed early in the morning—it was something else to be stuck in a strange place with a girl from a whole other race. And Mary, that's my mother, she was right. Every now and then she would stop dancing long enough to tell me something important and one of the things she said was that they never washed their hair and they smelled funny. Roberta sure did. Smell funny, I mean. So when the Big Bozo (nobody ever called her Mrs. Itkin, just like nobody ever said St. Bonaventure)—when she said, "Twyla, this is Roberta. Roberta, this is Twyla. Make each other welcome," I said, "My mother won't like you putting me in here."

"Good," said Bozo. "Maybe then she'll come and take you home."

How's that for mean? If Roberta had laughed I would have killed her, but she didn't. She just walked over to the window and stood with her back to us.

"Turn around," said the Bozo. "Don't be rude. Now Twyla. Roberta. When you hear a loud buzzer, that's the call for dinner. Come down to the first floor. Any fights and no movie." And then, just to make sure we knew what we would be missing, "*The Wizard of Oz.*"

Roberta must have thought I meant that my mother would be mad about my being put in the shelter. Not about rooming with her, because as soon as Bozo left she came over to me and said, "Is your mother sick too?"

"No," I said. "She just likes to dance all night."

"Oh." She nodded her head and I liked the way she understood things so fast. So for the moment it didn't matter that we looked like salt and pepper standing there and that's what the other kids called us sometimes. We were eight years old and got F's all the time. Me because I couldn't remember what I read or what the teacher said. And Roberta because she couldn't read at all and didn't even listen to the teacher. She wasn't good at anything except jacks, at which she was a killer: pow scoop pow scoop pow scoop.

We didn't like each other all that much at first, but nobody else wanted to play with us because we weren't real orphans with beautiful dead parents in the sky. We were dumped. Even the New York City Puerto Ricans and the upstate Indians ignored us. All kinds of kids were in there, black ones, white ones, even two Koreans. The food was good, though. At least I thought so. Roberta hated it and left whole pieces of things on her plate: Spam, Salisbury steak— even Jell-O with fruit cocktail in it—and she didn't care if I ate what she wouldn't. Mary's idea of supper was popcorn and a can of Yoo-hoo. Hot mashed potatoes and two weenies was like Thanksgiving for me.

It really wasn't bad, St. Bonny's. The big girls on the second floor pushed us around now and then. But that was all. They wore lipstick and eyebrow pencil and wobbled their knees while they watched TV. Fifteen, sixteen, even, some of them were. They were put-out girls, scared runaways most of them. Poor little girls who fought their uncles off but looked tough to us, and mean. God did they look mean. The staff tried to keep them separate from the younger children, but sometimes they caught us watching them in the orchard where they played radios and danced with each other. They'd light out after us and pull our hair or twist our arms. We were scared of them, Roberta and me, but neither of us wanted the other one to know it. So we got a good list of dirty names we could shout back when we ran from them through the orchard. I used to dream a lot and almost always the orchard was there. Two acres, four maybe, of these little apple trees. Hundreds of them. Empty and crooked like beggar women when I first came to St. Bonny's but fat with flowers when I left. I don't know why I dreamt about that orchard so much. Nothing really happened there. Nothing all that important, I mean. Just the big girls dancing and playing the radio. Roberta and me watching. Maggie fell down there once. The kitchen woman with legs like parentheses. And the big girls laughed at her. We should have helped her up, I know, but we were scared of those girls with lipstick and eyebrow pencil. Maggie couldn't talk. The kids said she had her tongue cut out, but I think she was just born that way: mute. She was old and sandy colored and she worked in the kitchen. I don't know if she was nice or not. I just remember her legs like parentheses and how she rocked when she walked. She worked from early in the morning till two o'clock, and if she was late, if she had too much cleaning and didn't get out till two fifteen or so, she'd cut through the orchard so she wouldn't miss her bus and have to wait another hour. She wore this really stupid little hat—a kid's hat with earflaps—and she wasn't much taller than we were. A really awful little hat. Even for a mute, it was dumb—dressing like a kid and never saying anything at all.

"But what about if somebody tries to kill her?" I used to wonder about that. "Or what if she wants to cry? Can she cry?"

"Sure," Roberta said. "But just tears. No sounds come out."

"She can't scream?"

"Nope. Nothing."

"Can she hear?"

"I guess."

"Let's call her," I said. And we did.

"Dummy! Dummy!" She never turned her head.

"Bow legs! Bow legs!" Nothing. She just rocked on, the chin straps of her baby-boy hat swaying from side to side. I think we were wrong. I think she could hear and didn't let on. And it shames me even now to think there was somebody in there after all who heard us call her those names and couldn't tell on us.

We got along all right, Roberta and me. Changed beds every night, got F's in civics and communication skills and gym. The Bozo was disappointed in us, she said. Out of 130 of us state cases, 90 were under twelve. Almost all were real orphans with beautiful dead parents in the sky. We were the only ones dumped and the only ones with F's in three classes including gym. So we got along—what with her leaving whole pieces of things on her plate and being nice about not asking questions.

I think it was the day before Maggie fell down that we found out our mothers were coming to visit us on the same Sunday. We had been at the shelter twenty-eight days (Roberta twenty-eight and a half) and this was their first visit with us. Our mothers would come at ten o'clock, in time for chapel, then lunch with us in the teachers' lounge. I thought if my dancing mother met her sick mother it might be good for her. And Roberta thought her sick mother would get a big bang out of a dancing one. We got excited about it and curled each other's hair. After breakfast we sat on the bed watching the road from the window. Roberta's socks were still wet. She washed them the night before and put them on the radiator to dry. They hadn't, but she put them on anyway because their tops were so pretty scalloped in pink. Each of us had a purple construction-paper basket that we had made in craft class. Mine had a yellow crayon rabbit on it. Roberta's had eggs with wiggly lines of color. Inside were cellophane grass and just the jelly beans because I'd eaten the two marshmallow eggs they gave us. The Big Bozo came herself to get us. Smiling she told us we looked very nice and to come downstairs. We were so surprised by the smile we'd never seen before, neither of us moved.

"Don't you want to see your mommies?"

I stood up first and spilled the jelly beans all over the floor. Bozo's smile disappeared while we scrambled to get the candy up off the floor and put it back in the grass.

She escorted us downstairs to the first floor, where the other girls were lining up to file into the chapel. A bunch of grown-ups stood to one side. Viewers mostly. The old biddies who wanted servants and the fags who wanted company looking for children they might want to adopt. Once in a while a grandmother. Almost never anybody young or anybody whose face wouldn't scare you in the night. Because if any of the real orphans had young relatives they wouldn't be real orphans. I saw Mary right away. She had on those green slacks I hated and hated even more now because didn't she know we were going to chapel? And that fur jacket with the pocket linings so ripped she had to pull to get her hands out of them. But her face was pretty—like always, and she smiled and waved like she was the little girl looking for her mother—not me.

I walked slowly, trying not to drop the jelly beans and hoping the paper handle would hold. I had to use my last Chiclet because by the time I finished cutting everything out, all the Elmer's was gone. I am left-handed and the scissors never worked for me. It didn't matter, though; I might just as well have chewed the gum. Mary dropped to her knees and grabbed me, mashing the basket, the jelly beans, and the grass into her ratty fur jacket.

"Twyla, baby. Twyla, baby!"

I could have killed her. Already I heard the big girls in the orchard the next time saying, "Twyyyyyla, baby!" But I couldn't stay mad at Mary while she was smiling and hugging me and smelling of Lady Esther dusting powder. I wanted to stay buried in her fur all day.

To tell the truth I forgot about Roberta. Mary and I got in line for the traipse into chapel and I was feeling proud because she looked so beautiful even in those ugly green slacks that made her behind stick out. A pretty mother on earth is better than a beautiful dead one in the sky even if she did leave you all alone to go dancing.

I felt a tap on my shoulder, turned, and saw Roberta smiling. I smiled back, but not too much lest somebody think this visit was the biggest thing that ever happened in my life. Then Roberta said, "Mother, I want you to meet my roommate, Twyla. And that's Twyla's mother."

I looked up it seemed for miles. She was big. Bigger than any man and on her chest was the biggest cross I'd ever seen. I swear it was six inches long each way. And in the crook of her arm was the biggest Bible ever made.

Mary, simpleminded as ever, grinned and tried to yank her hand out of the pocket with the raggedy lining—to shake hands, I guess. Roberta's mother looked down at me and then looked down at Mary too. She didn't say anything, just grabbed Roberta with her Bible-free hand and stepped out of line, walking quickly to the rear of it. Mary was still grinning because she's not too swift when it comes to what's really going on. Then this light bulb goes off in her head and she says, "That bitch!" really loud and us almost in the chapel now. Organ music whining; the Bonny Angels singing sweetly. Everybody in the world turned around to look. And Mary would have kept it up—kept calling names if I hadn't squeezed her hand as hard as I could. That helped a little, but she still twitched and crossed and uncrossed her legs all through service. Even groaned a couple of times. Why did I think she would come there and act right? Slacks. No hat like the grandmothers and viewers, and groaning all the while. When we stood for hymns she kept her mouth shut. Wouldn't even look at the words on the page. She actually reached in her purse for a mirror to check her lipstick. All I could think of was that she really needed to be killed. The sermon lasted a year, and I knew the real orphans were looking smug again.

We were supposed to have lunch in the teachers' lounge, but Mary didn't bring anything, so we picked fur and cellophane grass off the mashed jelly beans and ate them. I could have killed her. I sneaked a look at Roberta. Her mother had brought chicken legs and ham sandwiches and oranges and a whole box of chocolate-covered grahams. Roberta drank milk from a thermos while her mother read the Bible to her.

Things are not right. The wrong food is always with the wrong people. Maybe that's why I got into waitress work later—to match up the right people with the right food. Roberta just let those chicken legs sit there, but she did bring a stack of grahams up to me later when the visit was over. I think she was sorry that her mother would not shake my mother's hand. And I liked that and I liked the fact that she didn't say a word about Mary groaning all the way through the service and not bringing any lunch.

Roberta left in May when the apple trees were heavy and white. On her last day we went to the orchard to watch the big girls smoke and dance by the radio. It didn't matter that they said, "Twyyyyyla, baby." We sat on the ground and breathed. Lady Esther. Apple blossoms. I still go soft when I smell one or the other. Roberta was going home. The big cross and the big Bible was coming to get her and she seemed sort of glad and sort of not. I thought I would die in that room of four beds without her and I knew Bozo had plans to move some other dumped kid in there with me. Roberta promised to write every day, which was really sweet of her because she couldn't read a lick so how could she write anybody. I would have drawn pictures and sent them to her but she never gave me her address. Little by little she faded. Her wet socks with the pink scalloped tops and her big serious-looking eyes—that's all I could catch when I tried to bring her to mind.

I WAS WORKING behind the counter at the Howard Johnson's on the Thruway just before the Kingston exit. Not a bad job. Kind of a long ride from Newburgh, but okay once I got there. Mine was the second night shift, eleven to seven. Very light until a Greyhound checked in for breakfast around six thirty. At that hour the sun was all the way clear of the hills behind the restaurant. The place looked better at night—more like shelter—but I loved it when the sun broke in, even if it did show all the cracks in the vinyl and the speckled floor looked dirty no matter what the mop boy did.

It was August and a bus crowd was just unloading. They would stand around a long while: going to the john, and looking at gifts and junk-for-sale machines, reluctant to sit down so soon. Even to eat. I was trying to fill the coffeepots and get them all situated on the electric burners when I saw her. She was sitting in a booth smoking a cigarette with two guys smothered in head and facial hair. Her own hair was so big and wild I could hardly see her face. But the eyes. I would know them anywhere. She had on a powder-blue halter and shorts outfit and earrings the size of bracelets. Talk about lipstick and eyebrow pencil. She made the big girls look like nuns. I couldn't get off the counter until seven o'clock, but I kept watching the booth in case they got up to leave before that. My replacement was on time for a change, so I counted and stacked my receipts as fast as I could and signed off. I walked over to the booths, smiling and wondering if she would remember me. Or even if she wanted to remember me. Maybe she didn't want to be reminded of St. Bonny's or to have anybody know she was ever there. I know I never talked about it to anybody.

I put my hands in my apron pockets and leaned against the back of the booth facing them.

"Roberta? Roberta Fisk?"

She looked up. "Yeah?"

"Twyla."

She squinted for a second and then said, "Wow."

"Remember me?"

"Sure. Hey. Wow."

"It's been a while," I said, and gave a smile to the two hairy guys.

"Yeah. Wow. You work here?"

"Yeah," I said. "I live in Newburgh."

"Newburgh? No kidding?" She laughed then a private laugh that included the guys but only the guys, and they laughed with her. What could I do but laugh too and wonder why I was standing there with my knees showing out from under that uniform. Without looking I could see the blue and white triangle on my head, my hair shapeless in a net, my ankles thick in white oxfords. Nothing could have been less sheer than my stockings. There was this silence that came down right after I laughed. A silence it was her turn to fill up. With introductions, maybe, to her boyfriends or an invitation to sit down and have a Coke. Instead she lit a cigarette off the one she'd just finished and said, "We're on our way to the Coast. He's got an appointment with Hendrix."

She gestured casually toward the boy next to her.

"Hendrix? Fantastic," I said. "Really fantastic. What's she doing now?"

Roberta coughed on her cigarette and the two guys rolled their eyes up at the ceiling.

"Hendrix. Jimi Hendrix, asshole. He's only the biggest— Oh, wow. Forget it."

I was dismissed without anyone saying goodbye, so I thought I would do it for her.

"How's your mother?" I asked. Her grin cracked her whole face. She swallowed. "Fine," she said. "How's yours?"

"Pretty as a picture," I said and turned away. The backs of my knees were damp. Howard Johnson's really was a dump in the sunlight.

James is as comfortable as a house slipper. He liked my cooking and I liked his big loud family. They have lived in Newburgh all of their lives and talk about it the way people do who have always known a home. His grandmother is a porch swing older than his father and when they talk about streets and avenues and buildings they call them names they no longer have. They still call the A&P Rico's because it stands on property once a mom and pop store owned by Mr. Rico. And they call the new community college Town Hall because it once was. My mother-in-law puts up jelly and cucumbers and buys butter wrapped in cloth from a dairy. James and his father talk about fishing and baseball and I can see them all together on the Hudson in a raggedy skiff. Half the population of Newburgh is on welfare now, but to my husband's family it was still some upstate paradise of a time long past. A time of icehouses and vegetable wagons, coal furnaces and children weeding gardens. When our son was born my mother-in-law gave me the crib blanket that had been hers.

But the town they remembered had changed. Something quick was in the air. Magnificent old houses, so ruined they had become shelter for squatters and rent risks, were bought and renovated. Smart IBM people moved out of their suburbs back into the city and put shutters up and herb gardens in their backyards. A brochure came in the mail announcing the opening of a Food Emporium. Gourmet food it said—and listed items the rich IBM crowd would want. It was located in a new mall at the edge of town and I drove out to shop there one day—just to see.

It was late in June. After the tulips were gone and the Queen Elizabeth roses were open everywhere. I trailed my cart along the aisle tossing in smoked oysters and Robert's sauce and things I knew would sit in my cupboard for years. Only when I found some Klondike ice cream bars did I feel less guilty about spending James's fireman's salary so foolishly. My father-in-law ate them with the same gusto little Joseph did.

Waiting in the checkout line I heard a voice say, "Twyla!"

The classical music piped over the aisles had affected me and the woman leaning toward me was dressed to kill. Diamonds on her hand, a smart white summer dress. "I'm Mrs. Benson," I said.

"Ho. Ho. The Big Bozo," she sang.

For a split second I didn't know what she was talking about. She had a bunch of asparagus and two cartons of fancy water.

"Roberta!"

"Right."

"For heaven's sake. Roberta."

"You look great," she said.

"So do you. Where are you? Here? In Newburgh?"

"Yes. Over in Annandale."

I was opening my mouth to say more when the cashier called my attention to her empty counter.

"Meet you outside." Roberta pointed her finger and went into the express line.

I placed the groceries and kept myself from glancing around to check Roberta's progress. I remembered Howard Johnson's and looking for a chance to speak only to be greeted with a stingy "wow." But she was waiting for me and her huge hair was sleek now, smooth around a small, nicely shaped head. Shoes, dress, everything lovely and summery and rich. I was dying to know what happened to her, how she got from Jimi Hendrix to Annandale, a neighborhood full of doctors and IBM executives. Easy, I thought. Everything is so easy for them. They think they own the world.

"How long?" I asked her. "How long have you been here?"

"A year. I got married to a man who lives here. And you, you're married too, right? Benson, you said."

"Yeah. James Benson."

"And is he nice?"

"Oh, is he nice?"

"Well, is he?" Roberta's eyes were steady as though she really meant the question and wanted an answer.

"He's wonderful, Roberta. Wonderful."

"So you're happy."

"Very."

"That's good," she said and nodded her head. "I always hoped you'd be happy. Any kids? I know you have kids."

"One. A boy. How about you?"

"Four."

"Four?"

She laughed. "Step kids. He's a widower."

"Oh."

"Got a minute? Let's have a coffee."

I thought about the Klondikes melting and the inconvenience of going all the way to my car and putting the bags in the trunk. Served me right for buying all that stuff I didn't need. Roberta was ahead of me.

"Put them in my car. It's right here."

And then I saw the dark blue limousine.

"You married a Chinaman?"

"No," she laughed. "He's the driver."

"Oh, my. If the Big Bozo could see you now."

We both giggled. Really giggled. Suddenly, in just a pulse beat, twenty years disappeared and all of it came rushing back. The big girls (whom we called gar girls—Roberta's misheard word for the evil stone faces described in a civics class) there dancing in the orchard, the ploppy mashed potatoes, the double weenies, the Spam with pineapple. We went into the coffee shop holding on to one another and I tried to think why we were glad to see each other this time and not before. Once, twelve years ago, we passed like strangers. A black girl and a white girl meeting in a Howard Johnson's on the road and having nothing to say. One in a blue and white triangle waitress hat—the other on her way to see Hendrix. Now we were behaving like sisters separated for much too long. Those four short months were nothing in time. Maybe it was the thing itself. Just being there, together. Two little girls who knew what nobody else in the world knew—how not to ask questions. How to believe what had to be believed. There was politeness in that reluctance and generosity as well. Is your mother sick too? No, she dances all night. Oh—and an understanding nod.

We sat in a booth by the window and fell into rec-ollection like veterans.

"Did you ever learn to read?"

"Watch." She picked up the menu. "Special of the day. Cream of corn soup. Entrees. Two dots and a wriggly line. Quiche. Chef salad, scallops . . ."

I was laughing and applauding when the waitress came up.

"Remember the Easter baskets?"

"And how we tried to *introduce* them?"

"Your mother with that cross like two telephone poles."

"And yours with those tight slacks."

We laughed so loudly heads turned and made the laughter harder to suppress.

"What happened to the Jimi Hendrix date?"

Roberta made a blow-out sound with her lips.

"When he died I thought about you."

"Oh, you heard about him finally?"

"Finally. Come on, I was a small-town country waitress."

"And I was a small-town country dropout. God,

were we wild. I still don't know how I got out of there alive."

"But you did."

"I did. I really did. Now I'm Mrs. Kenneth Norton."

"Sounds like a mouthful."

"It is."

"Servants and all?"

Roberta held up two fingers.

"Ow! What does he do?"

"Computers and stuff. What do I know?"

"I don't remember a hell of a lot from those days, but Lord, St. Bonny's is as clear as daylight. Remember Maggie? The day she fell down and those gar girls laughed at her?"

Roberta looked up from her salad and stared at me. "Maggie didn't fall," she said.

"Yes, she did. You remember."

"No, Twyla. They knocked her down. Those girls pushed her down and tore her clothes. In the orchard."

"I don't— That's not what happened."

"Sure it is. In the orchard. Remember how scared we were?"

"Wait a minute. I don't remember any of that."

"And Bozo was fired."

"You're crazy. She was there when I left. You left before me."

"I went back. You weren't there when they fired Bozo."

"What?"

"Twice. Once for a year when I was about ten, another for two months when I was fourteen. That's when I ran away."

"You ran away from St. Bonny's?"

"I had to. What do you want? Me dancing in that orchard?"

"Are you sure about Maggie?"

"Of course I'm sure. You've blocked it, Twyla. It happened. Those girls had behavior problems, you know."

"Didn't they, though. But why can't I remember the Maggie thing?"

"Believe me. It happened. And we were there."

"Who did you room with when you went back?" I asked her as if I would know her. The Maggie thing was troubling me.

"Creeps. They tickled themselves in the night."

My ears were itching and I wanted to go home

suddenly. This was all very well but she couldn't just comb her hair, wash her face, and pretend everything was hunky-dory. After the Howard Johnson's snub. And no apology. Nothing.

"Were you on dope or what that time at Howard Johnson's?" I tried to make my voice sound friendlier than I felt.

"Maybe, a little. I never did drugs much. Why?"

"I don't know; you acted sort of like you didn't want to know me then."

"Oh, Twyla, you know how it was in those days: black-white. You know how everything was."

But I didn't know. I thought it was just the opposite. Busloads of blacks and whites came into Howard Johnson's together. They roamed together then: students, musicians, lovers, protesters. You got to see everything at Howard Johnson's and blacks were very friendly with whites in those days. But sitting there with nothing on my plate but two hard tomato wedges wondering about the melting Klondikes it seemed childish remembering the slight. We went to her car, and with the help of the driver, got my stuff into my station wagon.

"We'll keep in touch this time," she said.

"Sure," I said. "Sure. Give me a call."

"I will," she said, and then just as I was sliding behind the wheel, she leaned into the window. "By the way. Your mother. Did she ever stop dancing?"

I shook my head. "No. Never."

Roberta nodded.

"And yours? Did she ever get well?"

She smiled a tiny sad smile. "No. She never did. Look, call me, okay?"

"Okay," I said, but I knew I wouldn't. Roberta had messed up my past somehow with that business about Maggie. I wouldn't forget a thing like that. Would I?

STRIFE CAME TO US that fall. At least that's what the paper called it. Strife. Racial strife. The word made me think of a bird—a big shrieking bird out of 1,000,000,000 BC. Flapping its wings and cawing. Its eye with no lid always bearing down on you. All day it screeched and at night it slept on the rooftops. It woke you in the morning and from the *Today* show to the eleven o'clock news it kept you an awful company. I couldn't figure it out from one day to the next. I knew I was supposed to feel something strong, but I didn't know what, and James wasn't any help. Joseph was on the list of kids to be transferred from the junior high school to another one at some far-out-of-the-way place and I thought it was a good thing until I heard it was a bad thing. I mean I didn't know. All the schools seemed dumps to me, and the fact that one was nicer looking didn't hold much weight. But the papers were full of it and then the kids began to get jumpy. In August, mind you. Schools weren't even open yet. I thought Joseph might be frightened to go over there, but he didn't seem scared so I forgot about it, until I found myself driving along Hudson Street out there by the school they were trying to integrate and saw a line of women marching. And who do you suppose was in line, big as life, holding a sign in front of her bigger than her mother's cross? MOTHERS HAVE RIGHTS TOO! it said.

I drove on, and then changed my mind. I circled the block, slowed down, and honked my horn.

Roberta looked over and when she saw me she waved. I didn't wave back, but I didn't move either. She handed her sign to another woman and came over to where I was parked.

"Hi."

"What are you doing?"

"Picketing. What's it look like?"

"What for?"

"What do you mean, 'What for?' They want to take my kids and send them out of the neighborhood. They don't want to go."

"So what if they go to another school? My boy's being bussed too, and I don't mind. Why should you?"

"It's not about us, Twyla. Me and you. It's about our kids."

"What's more us than that?"

"Well, it is a free country."

"Not yet, but it will be."

"What the hell does that mean? I'm not doing anything to you."

"You really think that?"

"I know it."

"I wonder what made me think you were different."

"I wonder what made me think you were different."

"Look at them," I said. "Just look. Who do they think they are? Swarming all over the place like they own it. And now they think they can decide where my child goes to school. Look at them, Roberta. They're Bozos."

Roberta turned around and looked at the women. Almost all of them were standing still now, waiting. Some were even edging toward us. Roberta looked at me out of some refrigerator behind her eyes. "No, they're not. They're just mothers."

"And what am I? Swiss cheese?"

"I used to curl your hair."

"I hated your hands in my hair."

The women were moving. Our faces looked mean to them of course and they looked as though they could not wait to throw themselves in front of a police car, or better yet, into my car and drag me away by my ankles. Now they surrounded my car and gently, gently began to rock it. I swayed back and forth like a sideways yo-yo. Automatically I reached for Roberta, like the old days in the orchard when they saw us watching them and we had to get out of there, and if one of us fell the other pulled her up and if one of us was caught the other stayed to kick and scratch, and neither would leave the other behind. My arm shot out of the car window but no receiving hand was there. Roberta was looking at me sway from side to side in the car and her face was still. My purse slid from the car seat down under the dashboard. The four policemen who had been drinking Tab in their car finally got the message and strolled over, forcing their way through the women. Quietly, firmly they spoke. "Okay, ladies. Back in line or off the streets."

Some of them went away willingly; others had to be urged away from the car doors and the hood. Roberta didn't move. She was looking steadily at me. I was fumbling to turn on the ignition, which wouldn't catch because the gearshift was still in drive. The seats of the car were a mess because the swaying had thrown my grocery coupons all over it and my purse was sprawled on the floor.

"Maybe I am different now, Twyla. But you're not. You're the same little state kid who kicked a poor old black lady when she was down on the ground. You kicked a black lady and you have the nerve to call me a bigot."

The coupons were everywhere and the guts of my purse were bunched under the dashboard. What was she saying? Black? Maggie wasn't black.

"She wasn't black," I said.

"Like hell she wasn't, and you kicked her. We both did. You kicked a black lady who couldn't even scream."

"Liar!"

"You're the liar! Why don't you just go on home and leave us alone, huh?"

She turned away and I skidded away from the curb.

THE NEXT MORNING I went into the garage and cut the side out of the carton our portable TV had come in. It wasn't nearly big enough, but after a while I had a decent sign: red spray-painted letters on a white background: AND SO DO CHILDREN****. I meant just to go down to the school and tack it up somewhere so those cows on the picket line across the street could see it, but when I got there, some ten or so others had already assembled protesting the cows across the street. Police permits and everything. I got in line and we strutted in time on our side while Roberta's group strutted on theirs. That first day we were all dignified, pretending the other side didn't exist. The second day there was name calling and finger gestures. But that was about all. People changed signs from time to time, but Roberta never did and neither did I. Actually my sign didn't make sense without Roberta's. "And so do children what?" one of the women on my side asked me. "Have rights," I said, as though it was obvious.

Roberta didn't acknowledge my presence in any way and I got to thinking maybe she didn't know I was there. I began to pace myself in the line, jostling people one minute and lagging behind the next, so Roberta and I could reach the end of our respective lines at the same time and there would be a moment in our turn when we would face each other. Still, I couldn't tell whether she saw me and knew my sign was for her. The next day I went early before we were scheduled to assemble. I waited until she got there before I exposed my new creation. As soon as she hoisted her MOTHERS HAVE RIGHTS TOO! I began to wave my new one, which said, HOW WOULD YOU KNOW? I know she saw that one, but I had gotten addicted now. My signs got crazier each day, and the women on my side decided that I was a kook. They couldn't make heads or tails out of my brilliant screaming posters.

I brought a painted sign in queenly red with huge black letters that said, IS YOUR MOTHER WELL? Roberta took her lunch break and didn't come back for the rest of the day or any day after. Two days later I stopped going too and couldn't have been missed because nobody understood my signs anyway.

It was a nasty six weeks. Classes were suspended and Joseph didn't go to anybody's school until October. The children—everybody's children—soon got bored with that extended vacation they thought was going to be so great. They looked at TV until their eyes flattened. I spent a couple of mornings tutoring my son, as the other mothers said we should. Twice I opened a text from last year that he had never turned in. Twice he yawned in my face. Other mothers organized living room sessions so the kids would keep up. None of the kids could concentrate so they drifted back to *The Price Is Right* and *The Brady Bunch*. When the school finally opened there were fights once or twice and some sirens roared through the streets every once in a while. There were a lot of photographers from Albany. And just when ABC was about to send up a news crew, the kids settled down like nothing in the world had happened. Joseph

hung my HOW WOULD YOU KNOW? sign in his bed-
room. I don't know what became of AND SO DO CHIL-
DREN****. I think my father-in-law cleaned some
fish on it. He was always puttering around in our
garage. Each of his five children lived in Newburgh
and he acted as though he had five extra homes.

I couldn't help looking for Roberta when Joseph
graduated from high school, but I didn't see her. It
didn't trouble me much what she had said to me in
the car. I mean the kicking part. I know I didn't do
that, I couldn't do that. But I was puzzled by her telling me Maggie was black. When I thought about it
I actually couldn't be certain. She wasn't pitch-black,
I knew, or I would have remembered that. What I
remember was the kiddie hat, and the semicircle
legs. I tried to reassure myself about the race thing
for a long time until it dawned on me that the truth
was already there, and Roberta knew it. I didn't kick
her; I didn't join in with the gar girls and kick that
lady, but I sure did want to. We watched and never
tried to help her and never called for help. Maggie
was my dancing mother. Deaf, I thought, and dumb.
Nobody inside. Nobody who would hear you if you
cried in the night. Nobody who could tell you any-

thing important that you could use. Rocking, dancing, swaying as she walked. And when the gar girls pushed her down, and started roughhousing, I knew she wouldn't scream, couldn't—just like me and I was glad about that.

We decided not to have a tree, because Christmas would be at my mother-in-law's house, so why have a tree at both places? Joseph was at SUNY New Paltz and we had to economize, we said. But at the last minute, I changed my mind. Nothing could be that bad. So I rushed around town looking for a tree, something small but wide. By the time I found a place, it was snowing and very late. I dawdled like it was the most important purchase in the world and the tree man was fed up with me. Finally I chose one and had it tied onto the trunk of the car. I drove away slowly because the sand trucks were not out yet and the streets could be murder at the beginning of a snowfall. Downtown the streets were wide and rather empty except for a cluster of people coming out of the Newburgh Hotel. The one hotel in town that wasn't built out of cardboard and Plexiglas. A party, probably. The men huddled in the snow were dressed in tails and the women had on furs. Shiny things glittered from underneath their coats. It made me tired to look at them. Tired, tired, tired. On the next corner was a small diner with loops and loops of paper bells in the window. I stopped the car and went in. Just for a cup of coffee and twenty minutes of peace before I went home and tried to finish everything before Christmas Eve.

"Twyla?"

There she was. In a silvery evening gown and dark fur coat. A man and another woman were with her, the man fumbling for change to put in the cigarette machine. The woman was humming and tapping on the counter with her fingernails. They all looked a little bit drunk.

"Well. It's you."

"How are you?"

I shrugged. "Pretty good. Frazzled. Christmas and all."

"Regular?" called the woman from the counter.

"Fine," Roberta called back and then, "Wait for me in the car."

She slipped into the booth beside me. "I have to tell you something, Twyla. I made up my mind if I ever saw you again, I'd tell you."

"I'd just as soon not hear anything, Roberta. It doesn't matter now, anyway."

"No," she said. "Not about that."

"Don't be long," said the woman. She carried two regulars to go and the man peeled his cigarette pack as they left.

"It's about St. Bonny's and Maggie."

"Oh, please."

"Listen to me. I really did think she was black. I didn't make that up. I really thought so. But now I can't be sure. I just remember her as old, so old. And because she couldn't talk—well, you know, I thought she was crazy. She'd been brought up in an institution like my mother was and like I thought I would be too. And you were right. We didn't kick her. It was the gar girls. Only them. But, well, I wanted to. I really wanted them to hurt her. I said we did it, too. You and me, but that's not true. And I don't want you to carry that around. It was just that I wanted to do it so bad that day—wanting to is doing it."

Her eyes were watery from the drinks she'd had, I guess. I know it's that way with me. One glass of wine and I start bawling over the littlest thing.

"We were kids, Roberta."

"Yeah. Yeah. I know, just kids."

"Eight."

"Eight."

"And lonely."

"Scared, too."

She wiped her cheeks with the heel of her hand and smiled. "Well, that's all I wanted to say."

I nodded and couldn't think of any way to fill the silence that went from the diner past the paper bells on out into the snow. It was heavy now. I thought I'd better wait for the sand trucks before starting home.

"Thanks, Roberta."

"Sure."

"Did I tell you, my mother, she never did stop dancing."

"Yes. You told me. And mine, she never got well." Roberta lifted her hands from the tabletop and covered her face with her palms. When she took them away she really was crying. "Oh shit, Twyla. Shit, shit, shit. What the hell happened to Maggie?"

TONI MORRISON is the author of eleven novels, from *The Bluest Eye* (1970) to *God Help the Child* (2015). She received the National Book Critics Circle Award, the Pulitzer Prize, and in 1993 the Nobel Prize in Literature. She died in 2019.

A NOTE ON THE TYPE

This book was set in Granjon, a type named in compliment to Robert Granjon, a type cutter and printer active in Antwerp, Lyons, Rome, and Paris from 1523 to 1590. Linotype Granjon was designed by George W. Jones, who based his drawings on a face used by Claude Garamond (ca. 1480–1561) in his beautiful French books.

Composed by North Market Street Graphics,
Lancaster, Pennsylvania

Printed and bound by Friesens,
Altona, Manitoba

Designed by Cassandra J. Pappas